ROOKIE
RUNNER

BY JAKE MADDOX

text by
Sarah Hannah Gómez

STONE ARCH BOOKS
a capstone imprint

Jake Maddox JV Boys books are published by
Stone Arch Books
a Capstone imprint
1710 Roe Crest Drive
North Mankato, Minnesota 56003
www.mycapstone.com

Cataloging-in-Publication Data is available on the Library of Congress website.
ISBN: 978-1-4965-6332-3 (library binding)
ISBN: 978-1-4965-6334-7 (paperback)
ISBN: 978-1-4965-6336-1 (eBook PDF)

Summary: When Alvin's sister lands the lead in the school play, his parents tell him he'll need
to find an after-school activity to keep him busy until they can pick up both kids. A fast runner,
Alvin would like to give track and field a try, but it's the wrong season and he reluctantly chooses
cross country instead. But there's more to running cross country than being fast. Alvin must learn
how to use patience and pacing, or he'll be left in the dust.

Designer: Charmaine Whitman

Photo Credits: Shutterstock: cluckva, 92–93 (background), trek6500, cover, back cover, chapter
openers, 1, 90

Printed and bound in the United States of America.
PA021

TABLE OF CONTENTS

CHAPTER 1
YASMIN'S NEWS 5

CHAPTER 2
ALVIN'S ACTIVITY 15

CHAPTER 3
FIRST DAY 21

CHAPTER 4
TIME TRIALS 29

CHAPTER 5
FORM AND PACE 39

CHAPTER 6
TRAINING TEAMS 47

CHAPTER 7
GAINING GROUND 57

CHAPTER 8
RUN FOR FUN 67

CHAPTER 9
CROSS-TRAINING 71

CHAPTER 10
FIRST RACE 79

CHAPTER 11
ALL IN 83

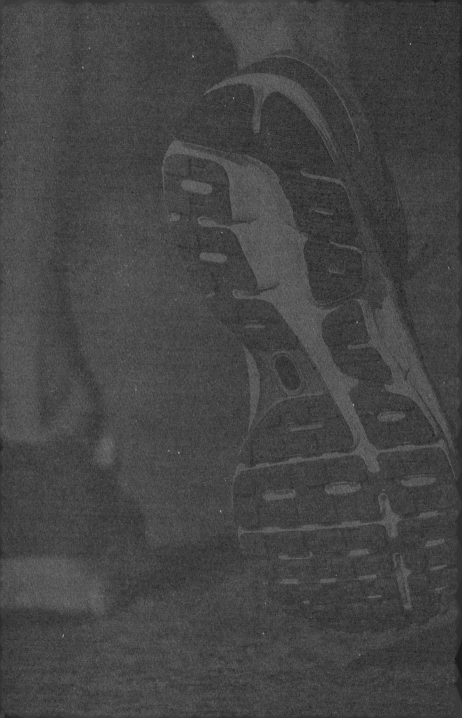

CHAPTER 1

YASMIN'S NEWS

At the end of the school day, Alvin Braga watched the school building empty from a tree branch near the bus line. Middle schoolers climbed into school buses, slid into their parents' cars, and hopped on their bicycles to go home.

Alvin looked back toward the school building, watching as two girls in particular came closer. He crouched down so they wouldn't see him.

Just as the girls walked under the tree, Alvin jumped off the branch and landed in front of them. "Boo!" he yelled.

They shrieked. One jumped in surprise. The other dropped a bag of candy she had been carrying, and the candies spilled out onto the dirt.

"Alvin! You jerk!" said the girl who dropped her candy. She was Alvin's twin sister, Yasmin. "I saved that from lunch."

Alvin shrugged. "Sorry," he said. "I just meant to surprise you. I didn't know you were carrying anything."

Yasmin rolled her eyes. "Sorry, Jessica," she said to the other girl Alvin had startled. "My brother can be so annoying."

"It's cool," Jessica said. "That's my bus. Gotta go!"

Yasmin waved goodbye and then turned back to her brother. "The snack bar's closed," she said. "There goes my chance for junk food today." Yasmin and Alvin's mom was a dentist, so they had to sneak candy if they wanted it.

"Sorry, Yas," Alvin said. Crouching down, he gathered up the candies from the dirt. He looked around. There was one garbage can a few feet away and one all the way down at the end of the block.

"Time me, Yas!" Alvin said. He took off running for the far one. He dumped the candies into the trash and turned right back around. His feet pounded into the dirt until he reached his sister and skidded to a stop.

"How fast was I?" Alvin asked.

"How should I know?" Yasmin replied.

"I wanted you to time me!" Alvin said.

"And I wanted to eat my candy before Dad came to pick us up," said Yasmin. "So I guess we're both going to be disappointed today."

Alvin frowned. *I'll just time myself,* he thought.

Telling himself to keep count in his head, he made a run for the garbage can again. When he returned to his starting point, he realized he had lost count as soon as he started running.

Before he could go for a third try, Yasmin nudged him. "There's Dad," she said.

Their father's car pulled up. The window rolled down. "Hey, kids!" their father said. "Get in."

As they pulled away from the curb, Dad asked, "So anything cool happen today?"

"Yes!" Yasmin shrieked. "But I want to wait to say anything until we get home. I want Mom to hear too."

"Well, OK! What about you, Alv?" Dad said. "Learn anything? Do anything? See anyone?"

Alvin shrugged and slumped back into the backseat.

"Can't see ya, buddy," Dad said, adjusting the rearview mirror.

"Nothing," Alvin said quietly.

"I find that hard to believe," Dad said. "Tell me something that was new to you today."

The rule was, you had to tell Mom and Dad at least one important thing about your day, and then you could be quiet if you wanted to.

"We finished a unit in science today," Alvin remembered. "Now that we've learned about heat and pressure, we're going to make our own hot-air balloons."

"That's amazing!" Dad said. "When I was in school, we didn't do anything nearly as fun. We would just read about hot-air balloons in a textbook. You're going to have a blast!"

"I guess," Alvin said, trying not to sound too excited. He smiled to himself, though. He *was* kind of excited about making a hot-air balloon. Not only would his fly high, but he would make sure it looked the best once it was up in the sky too.

Now that he had told Dad something about his day, Alvin could sit back while Yasmin chattered up in front. She always had a thousand things to say.

* * *

When they arrived home, Alvin dropped his backpack near the couch and made for his bedroom. Yasmin followed their parents to the kitchen, and Alvin could hear them start dinner.

He sat at his desk and pulled out some pencils from a drawer. Then he opened his sketchbook, ready to draw.

"Alvin, please move your backpack!" Mom called.

Alvin dropped his pencil and sighed. Back in the living room, he jumped over a side table, easily cleared it, and then slid across the tile to where his backpack lay.

"No sliding in sneakers!" Dad called out.

Alvin sighed again, picked up his bag, and headed back to his room. He tossed the backpack next to his bed and sat down again at his desk.

"Alvin, can you come in here?" Mom called from the kitchen.

He got up again and headed to the kitchen, walking this time. "Yeah?" he asked when he got there. Everyone was working on dinner: Yasmin was at the sink rinsing off vegetables, Dad was cutting up some chicken, and Mom was looking through a cabinet of pots and pans.

"Your sister says she has some news," Mom said. "And she wanted to tell the whole family at once."

"What is it, Yas?" Dad asked.

Yasmin turned from the sink, a huge grin on her face. "I got the lead in the seventh-grade play!" she exclaimed.

"That's wonderful!" said Mom.

"Congratulations!" Dad added.

Mom and Dad looked over at Alvin expectantly. "Congratulations, sis," he said, with a lot less enthusiasm than his parents. Yas was always getting big roles—in student council, in Science Olympics, and now in the play.

"Rehearsals are after school," Yasmin said. "Four days a week."

"Until when?" Dad asked.

"Five-thirty," said Yasmin.

"Wow, that's late," said Mom.

"We'll have to figure out some kind of arrangement for that," Dad said. "I can't drive to school twice in the afternoon to pick one of you up and then the other."

"Alvin, maybe you can join the play as well," Mom said.

"All the parts are cast," Yasmin said. "But I think the stage crew needs more people."

"No," Alvin said. "Just because we're twins doesn't mean we have to do all the same things."

"Of course not," Dad said. "Is there a different after-school activity you'd like to do?"

"I dunno," Alvin said.

"I suppose there's always the library," Mom said. "I know Ms. Martinez is there until five. It would mean you could get most of your homework done before you get home."

"Ugh," said Alvin. "I don't want to get out of school and have to keep doing schoolwork without a break."

"They're just ideas, Alvin," Mom said. "Why don't you ask around and see if there's something you would like to do? The school has lots of activities, and you're good at lots of things."

"Tons of things!" Dad agreed. "Let's check the school website after dinner. Maybe you'll find something you're interested in."

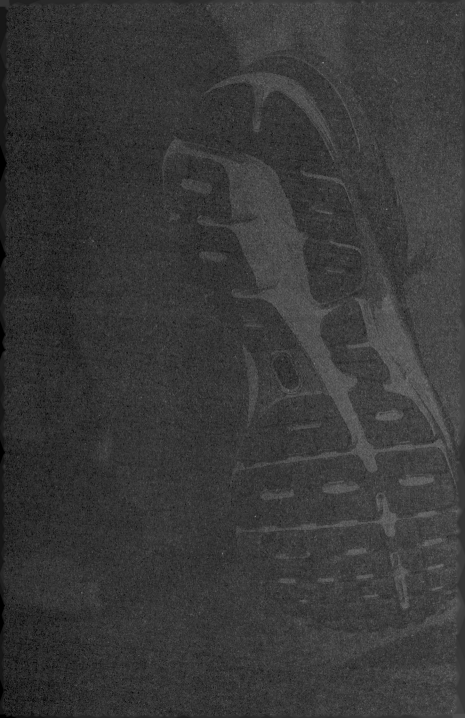

CHAPTER 2

ALVIN'S ACTIVITY

The rule was that if one twin helped get dinner ready, the other one had to do the dishes. Tonight it was Alvin's turn. When he had dried the last plate and wrung out the sponge, he went to the living room where Dad was sitting with his laptop.

Dad patted the space next to him on the couch. "Come on, Alv," he said. "Let's see what we can find." Alvin sat down and hugged a throw pillow to his chest. Dad navigated to the school's website and clicked on *EXTRACURRICULARS*. A long list of activities loaded.

"You let me know when something looks good," Dad said.

Alvin scanned the list. Tutoring was out. Drama was out. Photography sounded interesting, but as he read he realized it said it was canceled for the current school year. They hadn't found a new advisor for the club.

Alvin jiggled his leg and tapped the floor with his foot as he kept scrolling through. Chess club wouldn't work. He had tried chess once, but he didn't like how slow the game went. Alvin was not a fan of going slowly at anything.

Not dance. Not pottery. Not choir.

He sighed. There was nothing. He was going to be forced to do homework right after school while everyone else had fun.

"It's no use," he said. "I'm never going to find anything. I'm going to my room." He got up from the couch and tossed the pillow he had been holding at the easy chair across from him. He missed.

"Pick it up, Alv," Dad said. Alvin sighed again. Eyeing the distance between him and the pillow, Alvin took a breath and picked his knees up, jumping over the coffee table toward the easy chair. He *just* cleared it, by a mere couple of inches. If something had been on top of it, he would have knocked it over.

"Please don't do that," Mom said from behind him. She had come into the room and was looking over Dad's shoulder at the computer. "You make me so nervous, and that table is made of glass."

"You have to admit, it was a good jump," said Dad.

"Don't encourage him, Isaac!" Mom said.

"Alvin, do not do those *very impressive* jumps inside the house," Dad said. "Outdoors only."

Mom sighed, but she had a smile on her face.

"Hey, that's an idea!" Dad said. "Maybe there's a circus club. You can work on your tumbling and trapeze skills."

Mom snorted.

"You're a dork, Dad," said Alvin.

"You can't tell me that wouldn't be fun," Dad said.

"Sure," Alvin admitted. "But I don't think our school would have a circus club. You're not helping me find an activity."

"There's always the library," Dad said.

"I guess," Alvin grumbled.

"There may not be a circus club," Mom said. "But there must be something that will allow you to get all that energy out. What about track and field?"

That actually sounded like fun. "Yeah!" Alvin said. "Track and field."

"Good idea, but that's a spring sport," Dad said. He clicked around. "Here! I found the perfect thing. Cross country!"

"I dunno," Alvin said. "That sounds boring. All they do is . . . run. There's no jumping or throwing or sliding."

"I think cross country sounds great," Mom said. "You're fast, and you love to keep moving."

"Sounds like a winner," Dad added.

Alvin sighed. He didn't want to admit it, but his parents were right. He still wished he could try track and field, but cross country might be a good second. "OK," he said. "I'll try cross country."

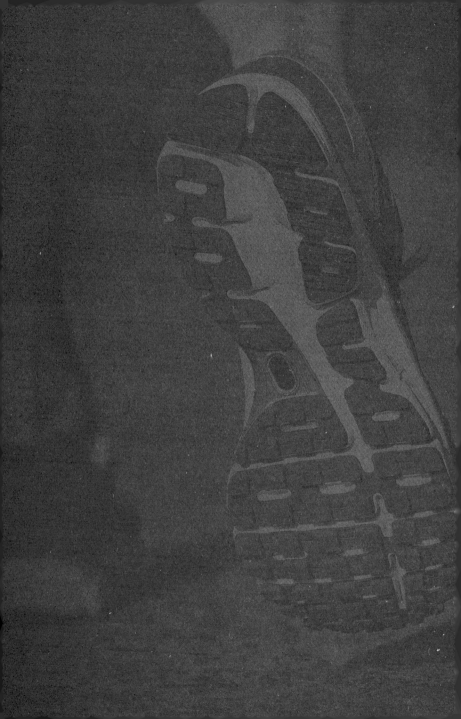

CHAPTER 3

FIRST DAY

When the last bell rang on Monday, Alvin headed out to the school field for the first day of cross country.

As he approached, he could see about twenty other kids out there waiting. He recognized a boy from science class, but he couldn't remember his name. Everyone took a seat in the grass.

Coach Henry, a tall man a little older than Alvin's parents, was pacing in front of them. He had a clipboard in one hand and a pencil in the other.

"Welcome, everyone," Coach Henry said. "I'm happy to see some returning faces from last season, and I'm excited to get to know the rest of you soon. Who's ready to start the season?"

Everyone cheered, even Alvin.

"Great!" Coach Henry said. "Let's get going."

Alvin began to get up from the grass, but then he realized everyone around him was staying seated. He plopped back down.

What else could they be doing? Alvin was ready to run. He knew everyone would be impressed with how fast he was.

"Now this," Coach Henry said, "is the most important bit." He pulled a sheet of paper off his clipboard and waved it in front of the team.

"This is your contract. I want you to take it, read it, and carefully consider it before you sign it," Coach said. "It's something you are agreeing to for the entire cross country season, and I take it very seriously. If you don't sign this contract, you can't be on the team."

Alvin looked in amazement. *A contract? Like real athletes?*

Some kids seemed unsurprised. Alvin figured they must have been the ones who had been on the team in the past. He caught the eye of a girl who looked equally shocked and overwhelmed. He saw another boy mouth "What?" to his friend, who mouthed "I know" back.

The coach continued, "I'll go over it today, but I want you to take it home and review it with your parents before you sign. I want them to know that you've committed to something really great, that you plan to work really hard on something this semester, even outside of your schoolwork. If you look over this and decide cross country's not for you, no hard feelings."

This is unbelievable, Alvin thought. *Considering it's a middle school sport, Coach Henry takes this really seriously. I just want to run!*

Coach Henry read out the contract, which was full of pledges not to miss a single practice (unless they were sick), to be responsible for getting themselves to meets, and to care for their bodies by eating well, stretching, taking rest days, and working hard.

It was a long list—the contract didn't just have rules about coming to practice on time and working hard. It also talked about cheering for your teammates, keeping your grades up, and many other things. At the end, Coach Henry said he wanted "scholar-athletes" on the team, meaning that you had to be responsible both in school and on the team.

Coach Henry was taking forever to finish talking. Alvin could see that many of the kids around him— his new teammates—were getting restless.

Finally, Coach Henry got to the end of the contract. Laying his clipboard in the grass, he unclipped the papers and handed a pile to the girl on his left and the boy on his right. They each took one and began passing the rest.

When Alvin got his, he unzipped his backpack and put the contract in without reading it. He would sign it when he got home.

"One more thing," Coach Henry said. "You should all have your health information on file with the school nurse. If you signed up for cross country before today, I already got it from the nurse. If you didn't, please tell me now so that I can be sure I make copies tomorrow. I also ask you each to give me a copy of your school schedule so that I can be in touch with your teachers."

He picked up the clipboard again and said, "Now, I'm going to call out the names of people whose information I do have to make sure you're here. Arianna?"

The girl Alvin had made eye contact with earlier answered. "Yup!"

"Jake?"

"Here."

Coach Henry continued to read off names, Alvin's among them. His mom had signed him up online the night before. The last name Coach Henry read was Emilio.

"Yeah," said a boy sitting in the front of the pack. Somebody whistled.

"This guy was runner-up for state champion last year," Coach Henry explained.

"Champion this year!" Emilio said. He pumped his fist.

"That's the goal," Coach Henry said. "I'd like to see quite a few champions and runners-up this season if we can. But what I'm really looking for is for each of you to have a baseline where you begin and a marked improvement by the end of the season. As long as you're moving up in your ability, that's a win for you and for me."

Alvin wondered how fast he would be by the end of the season. He was already starting out pretty fast.

"OK," Coach Henry said now. "Who's ready to run?"

Everyone cheered.

"Well, we have to wait until tomorrow," Coach Henry said. He chuckled. "For now, I'm going to let you go. See you tomorrow!"

People slowly got up and slung their backpacks on. Some looked happy to have dodged a practice, while others were clearly disappointed. As for Alvin, he sprinted his way to meet Dad and Yasmin at the car.

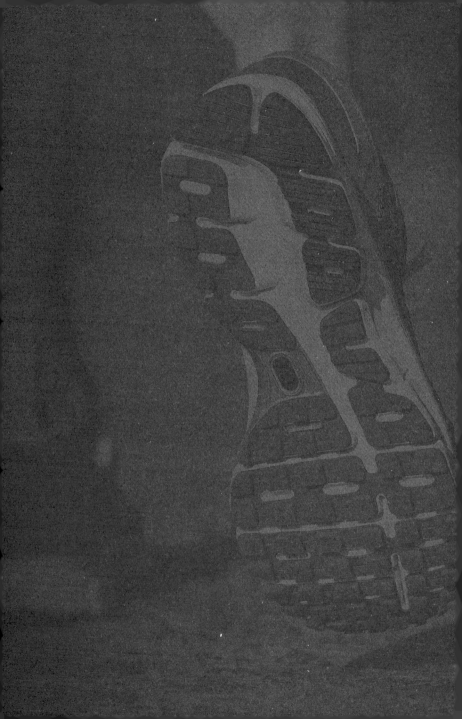

CHAPTER 4

TIME TRIALS

"Let's warm up."

It was the first real practice of the season. Alvin and the others had just turned in their signed contracts.

The team made a circle on the field. Coach Henry stood in the middle, demonstrating stretches as he called them out. Some had silly names, like Zombie Walk. For that one, they had to hold both arms out in front them while they alternated raising each leg, keeping the leg straight the whole time.

Others were more straightforward. For Knee Taps each runner alternated bringing one knee up as high as possible to tap it against the palm of one hand. Then they had something called the Duck Walk, where they squatted down and took steps forward. The exercise made Alvin's legs burn.

We haven't even started running yet and I'm already sweating! he thought.

Finally, they were done warming up. Coach Henry looked at his watch. "I want us to do time trials today," he said. "But first I want everyone to get to know each other, since we have a lot of new people on the team this year. If you were on the team last year, raise your hand."

About eight hands went up. "OK," he continued, "each of you buddy up with one or two new folks."

Alvin looked around at who might choose him. He didn't even know what grade everybody was in, though he could tell that guy Emilio was an eighth grader from how confident he was.

Would that kid from science class want to be his buddy? He looked like he knew lots of people already, and Alvin didn't want to seem desperate. But he also didn't want to be left out.

Someone tapped him on the shoulder. It was a girl who looked like she might have been an eighth grader too. "Want to join us?" she asked. "I'm Keisha."

"I'm Alvin," he replied.

"This is Arianna," Keisha said, pointing to the girl standing next to her.

"Hi," Arianna said.

Before they could say more, Coach Henry blew his whistle. "We're going to play a game of Follow the Leader within your small groups."

Follow the Leader? thought Alvin. *That's for babies. What does that have to do with running?*

"The leaders will start off running, with the followers running behind them. Then the leader will change what they're doing, and the followers have to switch as quickly as possible," Coach explained.

"You could start skipping, maybe, or running backward, or cartwheeling. Do whatever you like, as long as you keep moving and you stay safe, and feel free to use the entire field for this. When I blow my whistle, a different person will become the leader. Got it?"

Everyone shouted, "Yes!"

"Great! Here we go," Coach said, and he blew his whistle.

Keisha took off jogging, and Alvin and Arianna followed. Keisha looked back at them to see that they had fallen in line, and then she switched to a skip.

Arianna switched without missing a beat. Alvin shuffled for a moment before he skipped too. After a while, Keisha changed again and began hopping like a bunny. Arianna and Alvin also hopped.

When the whistle blew, Keisha called out Arianna's name. Arianna took her place in the front of the line. She held her arms out to the side and began running, dipping her arms side to side like an airplane.

The whistle blew again. It was Alvin's turn. He dropped his arms from the airplane he'd had them in and picked up his running speed. The girls behind him sped up as well. Then Alvin jumped forward. Keisha and Arianna did too.

Alvin ran and jumped again, this time clearing about four feet. The girls followed. He sprinted again and then jumped as far as he could. He looked behind him to see how far Keisha and Arianna could jump. They had both stopped in their tracks.

"No thanks, Alvin!" Arianna said.

"Yeah, this is cross country, not cross *jumping*," Keisha added.

"Fine," Alvin grumbled. "No more long jumps."

Continuing to face the girls, he began to jog backward. When they saw what he was doing, they turned their bodies away from him and jogged backward in the same direction.

Alvin was having fun moving backward. He was starting to think of what he could do next when . . .

CRACK! He collided with someone, and they both fell onto the ground. Alvin looked to see who he had run into.

It was Emilio. "Watch where you're going!" Emilio snarled.

"Sorry," Alvin mumbled.

"Just don't do it again." Emilio shot Alvin a look that said he meant business.

The whistle blew again. "Bring it in!" Coach called.

Alvin and Emilio scrambled to their feet and ran over to the coach.

Everyone was clustered together, some people jogging in place rather than standing still. Keisha was gathering her braids together and putting them into a ponytail.

"Are you here for practice or to fix your hair?" Emilio asked Keisha. He turned to the boy next to him. "Too bad the girls aren't as worried about their times as they are about their hair. The team would do a lot better."

Keisha rolled her eyes. "No need to worry about my time or my hair," Keisha said. "I've got both under control, Emilio." She walked away from the boys.

"I need your attention up here, folks," Coach Henry said. "Our other order of business today is time trials. You're going to do four laps. That's one mile. I'll time you all. Your final times will help me put you into smaller groups for training. I want you training with people who work at around the same pace as you."

"What if we get faster and want to change groups?" a boy named Mike asked.

"We'll do more time trials over the course of the season," Coach Henry said. "Nothing's set in stone."

Everyone lined up at the start. Coach Henry picked up the timer that hung around his neck. "Make sure you pace yourselves. Take your mark, get set, go!"

The group tore off, Alvin near the front of the pack. Now *this* was what he had been waiting for. He finally got to go fast! He was pulling ahead from the group and in first place.

In no time at all, he was making his way back to Coach Henry, and not a second too soon. He slowed down, breathing hard, and then stopped. "Phew!"

Coach Henry looked up from his clipboard. "Three to go, Alvin."

What? Alvin had been so ready to run he hadn't paid attention to Coach's instructions.

"Three more?" he asked.

"That's a mile," Coach replied.

"You mean I only ran a quarter mile? I'm dead," Alvin said, barely getting the words out between breaths.

"You shouldn't have gone all out on your first lap," Coach said. Alvin frowned.

Nearly everyone had passed Coach and Alvin and started their second lap. Alvin could hardly imagine doing three more laps. He had run so hard for his first one.

Emilio sailed by, not out of breath at all. "See ya," he said as he ran past.

"Get going, Mr. Braga," Coach said. "The clock's ticking."

Alvin sighed and began jogging again. He was so tired that by the end of his second lap, he was in last place.

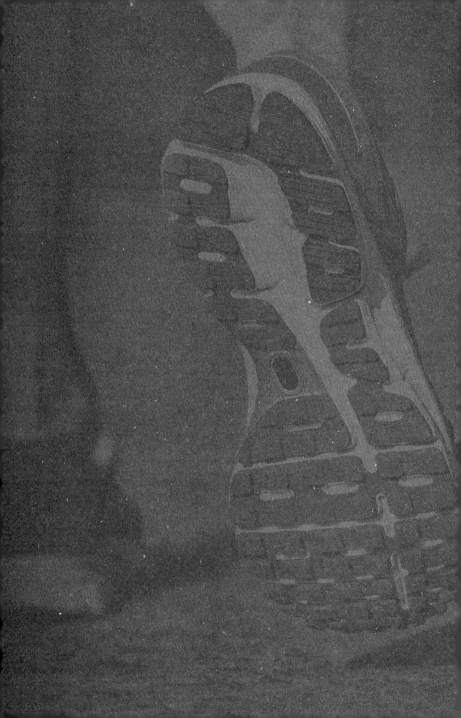

CHAPTER 5

FORM AND PACE

On Friday at dinner, Mom and Dad asked Alvin and Yasmin how their week had gone. Dad was passing the challah around the table. Alvin tore off a huge piece of the bread and stuffed the entire thing in his mouth.

"Alvin!" Mom said. "No one is taking your food away from you."

Alvin tore off one more chunk of the braided loaf before passing it to his sister.

"My week was great," Yasmin said. She neatly tore off a piece of challah and passed it to their mom. "I already have half of my lines memorized."

Alvin made a face. *Perfect Yasmin.*

"That's great, honey," Dad said.

"How was your week, Alvin?" Mom asked.

Alvin swallowed his challah. "Fine. We're almost done with our hot-air balloons in science," he said.

"I can't wait to hear how high they go," Mom said. "It sounds like you're really working hard in science."

"How's cross country?" Dad asked.

Alvin sighed. "It's really hard," he admitted. "I don't think Coach Henry likes me."

"What? Of course he does," Dad said. "What's not to like about you?"

"It's like he doesn't even care how good I am," Alvin said. "I'm super fast!"

"Cross country is more about the long haul," Dad added. "You might need to learn to slow down and pace yourself."

"Running slow is boring!" Alvin said.

"Not once you learn to do it right," Dad said. "Running long distances can give you a great feeling of accomplishment."

"I don't want to do it 'right' if that means I have to go slow," Alvin grumbled.

"You're not there to be the best sprinter, Alv," Mom said. "You're there to learn to run long distances—and to enjoy yourself!"

"And to make friends," Dad added. "It's a chance to meet people outside your classes, and even outside your grade."

"I don't think I'm going to make any new friends. I'm too different from everyone on the team," said Alvin. "They're happy running at a slow pace. I can go faster than all of them."

"Get over yourself, Alvin," Yasmin chimed in. "I don't think I'm better than everyone else just because I have the lead in the play. *Everyone* is responsible for making it the best play it can be."

"And since you can't sprint a whole cross country race," added Mom, "you are responsible for listening to your coach and running the way he wants you to. Learn from your coach."

Alvin groaned. He had joined because he wanted to be able to run the way *he* liked to run. Maybe he should find a different activity.

* * *

Mom and Dad wouldn't let Alvin drop cross country and sign up for something new. So for week two, he was still at practices.

"Today we're doing a long run," Coach Henry said after warm-ups. "It's all individual. I just want to get to know you as runners. For the rest of the time we have today, you're going to be running laps. I know it sounds boring, but I'll be able to keep an eye on you and give you pointers on your form and pace. If you think it's torture, don't worry. I'm going to run and be tortured myself!"

Everyone laughed.

Coach Henry pointed to the track. "Let's go!"

Alvin ran his first lap with no problem. It felt great to be on his own with the wind in his face as he pounded the field. He made it back to the start ahead of everyone, even Emilio. He went right into his second lap. Soon his coach was right in line with him.

"You're going too fast, Alvin," Coach Henry said. "You're going to burn out."

Alvin shook his head. "I love running," he said. "I can go forever like this."

"No, you can't. And that's not the point of cross country. One of the best things about it is that you get to look around you and enjoy the length of the run. I'll admit the view from campus and the repetitive runs around the track are not the most spectacular. But we'll be doing some runs off campus too."

"I can keep going," Alvin insisted.

"OK," Coach Henry agreed. "Let's see how it goes. But we need to work on your form too. You're leaning forward like a sprinter. Stand up straight and keep your chest open."

Alvin puffed his chest out like Emilio did whenever Coach Henry gave him a compliment.

"Not too much, though," the coach said. "It should feel natural, not awkward." Alvin relaxed a little. "There you go. Try to keep that position during your entire run."

Coach Henry jogged off to catch up with another group. *If he's running fast, why can't I?* thought Alvin.

He tried his best to keep his chest open like the coach had said. As he did so, he felt himself slowing down. Running the way Coach Henry had said was much harder.

Before long, Emilio and two other guys passed him by. "Too bad you can't compete with the girls' team," Emilio yelled. "They would be more your speed. You're so slow my grandma could beat you in a race."

Alvin boiled with anger, but he didn't say anything back. He went back to the way he preferred to run.

He leaned in like he was being pushed forward, speeding through the air rather than running on the earth. But no matter how hard he pushed, he didn't catch up with Emilio for the rest of practice.

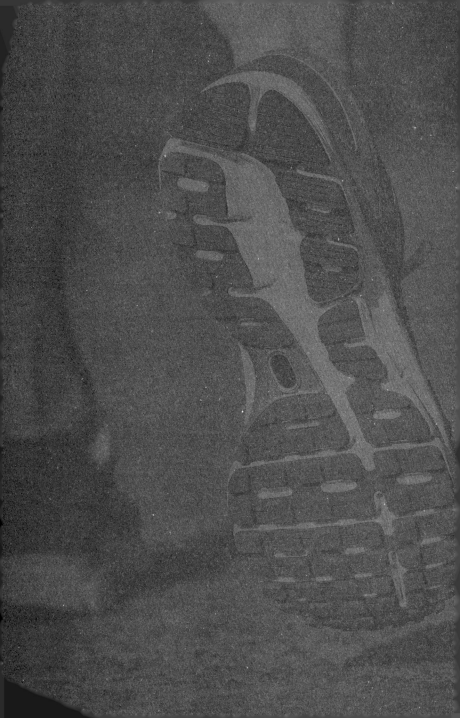

CHAPTER 6

TRAINING TEAMS

Coach Henry blew his whistle to quiet everyone down after warm-ups. "OK," he said. "Based on your time trials, I've put you into smaller training groups. That doesn't mean we're not all doing things as a team. But for certain activities you'll be with this group so you'll all be moving at more or less the same pace. All right, first group."

He began reading names off in groups of three or four. Alvin could tell the first group was the fastest, because Emilio was on it. Emilio puffed his chest out in pride.

Coach Henry called several more groups before he got to Alvin's name. Finally he called it out along with Arianna and a girl named Neela.

What? Me and two girls? Alvin thought. *How did I end up with two girls?*

Arianna seemed nice, but Alvin didn't want everyone to think he was a wimp. And he was *fast!* Shouldn't that count for something?

Coach called one more group after theirs. Alvin figured at least that meant his group wasn't the slowest, but he was still mad.

Coach Henry described the route they were going to take off campus. It was a loop through the neighborhood. They would run the loop twice for a total of four miles. Coach Henry would be running alongside the team, and three parents of runners were joining in as well.

Before Coach Henry blew his whistle again to let them head out, Alvin went over to talk to him.

"Am I in the right group?" he asked.

Coach Henry looked at his clipboard. "You, Arianna, and Neela. Yep."

"How come I'm with *girls?*" Alvin asked. "Shouldn't boys and girls run separately?"

"You will compete in separate groups, but we train as one team," Coach Henry said.

Alvin protested, "But some of the groups are all boys or all girls."

"Listen, nobody is better than anyone based on gender," said the coach. "You're in this group because I think you'll be able to stick together as a pack. You'll get to know each other, and I'm sure you'll be good friends by the end of the season."

"But—" Alvin started.

"No buts," said Coach Henry. "All the groups are final until we do another set of time trials in the middle of the season. And even then, everyone will have been working hard and improving their times, so you'll probably still be placed together. But it's the best place for you to be. Trust me."

"I'm a *boy*. I'll be competing against boys. I should be practicing with boys. If I'm not, why should I even be here?" Alvin whined.

"You signed a contract to be a scholar-athlete. If you are not able to meet all of the requirements, including that you see all of your teammates as fellow *athletes*, maybe you shouldn't be here after all," Coach said firmly.

Alvin was surprised at the suggestion he didn't belong on the team. Although he had been tempted to quit, he didn't like thinking that Coach might not want him to be there.

Still, it bothered him that he wasn't training with boys. "I'm just saying—" he began to protest.

"Mr. Braga, most of the team has already started on the loop," Coach said. "Your group is waiting for you. I suggest you go join them."

Alvin sighed. He looked over at Arianna and Neela. They were standing fairly close by, staring right at Alvin and Coach Henry. They had strange looks on their faces, like maybe they didn't want Alvin to join them either.

Alvin jogged over to catch up with them. They were moving slowly, but at least they weren't walking. Both girls had long hair, Arianna's thick and wavy brown, Neela's straight and almost black. Their ponytails bounced as they ran, matching each other in rhythm.

"Hey," Alvin said.

"Hi," both girls said back.

"Can we go a little faster?" Alvin asked.

"We have to run four miles today," Neela said. "I think we should conserve our energy."

Alvin frowned. This definitely wasn't the right group for him. They were slower than he was. "I knew I shouldn't have been put into a group with *girls*," Alvin huffed under his breath.

Arianna and Neela looked over at him as they jogged, keeping their pace. *Did they hear me?* Alvin thought.

* * *

Before the end of the first loop, Alvin's legs were burning. They hadn't taken a single break. He hoped they would at least stop for water when they made it back to campus.

Alvin's lower legs hurt in a way he'd never felt before. He wanted to suggest slowing down a bit, but he knew doing so would mean admitting that he was tired. He kept his mouth shut until they made it back to school and had finished their first loop.

Finally he couldn't do it anymore. "Can we take a walk break?" he asked. "My legs hurt."

"That works for me," Arianna said between breaths. "I'm pooped."

"Sure," Neela agreed.

The three slowed down. Arianna stopped for a moment, leaned over with her hands on her legs, and took some deep breaths. Neela was doing some kind of breathing exercise, rapidly breathing out through her mouth with a sound like a dog panting. Alvin took advantage of the break to stop and take some deep breaths as slowly as he could manage.

"I feel so out of breath after I've been running a while," Arianna said.

"You gotta make sure you are getting good deep breaths," said Neela. "Try taking in air for two steps and then breathing it out for two steps. It helps make sure your breathing isn't shallow."

"OK, thanks!" Arianna said. "I'll try it."

Neela turned to Alvin and asked, "Where do your legs hurt, Alvin?"

"Along the front here, by the shinbone," Alvin said. He pointed to the bottom part of his leg.

"Shin splints," Neela said. "I got those a lot last year. They're from running a lot more than you're used to. Ice your legs when you get home. As you run more, you'll stop getting them."

"Good, thanks. Were you on the team last year then?" Alvin asked. He had assumed his group mates were new, like him. But Neela seemed to know what she was doing.

"Yep," Neela said proudly. "I'm so much faster this year. Last year I needed a ton of walk breaks."

"What about you, Arianna?" Alvin asked.

"This is my first year," she answered. "Like you."

Emilio, Robert, and Oscar passed them by. "Lapped you!" Emilio shouted. "Have you three even left on your first loop yet?" Without waiting for an answer, the three of them easily ran past Alvin and his partners.

The comment stung Alvin, but the laughter amazed him. *I can't imagine having enough breath to laugh like that while I'm running*, he thought.

"I can't believe they're not even tired," Neela said. She didn't sound mad, either, only impressed.

"Me neither," Arianna said.

"We need to get going," Alvin said.

"There are still two miles to go," Arianna said. "We can't overdo it yet."

"Maybe we can push ourselves for just the last mile," Neela said.

"Fine," Alvin said. His legs told him to let Neela and Arianna set the pace, but a big part of him still wanted to go faster. He wanted to show Coach and Emilio and himself just what he could do.

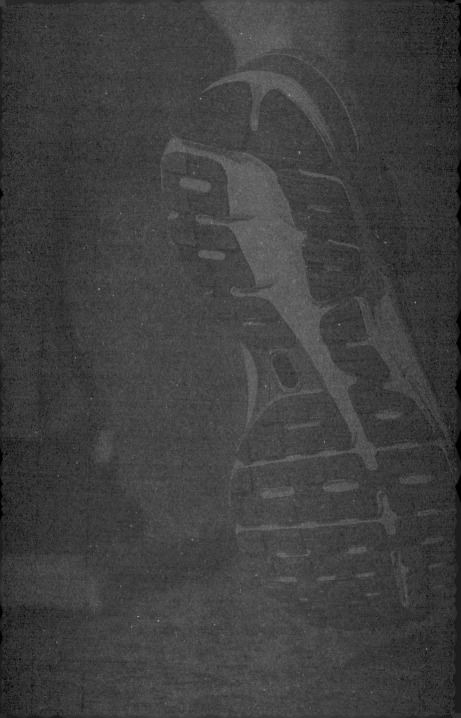

CHAPTER 7

GAINING GROUND

The team mostly did long runs that week, with one day of practicing on a small hill near their school. Alvin had never tried running at an incline before. He couldn't sprint, and he was one of the slowest on the team to complete all of his runs.

The next Monday, Coach Henry announced that they were doing fartleks. Alvin didn't know what those were. At least three people made farting noises with their armpits and most everyone else giggled. Arianna even snorted.

"Yeah, yeah," Coach Henry said. He seemed to know the jokes were coming. When the team quieted down, he continued. "Fartleks allow us to practice different paces and get to know how much energy it takes to sustain each one. This will come in handy during races so you know when to conserve your energy and when you need to push a little extra if you'd like to get ahead of someone."

That's what I'm talking about, thought Alvin. *I'm all about that extra push.*

"We have four different paces to work on," the coach continued. "First are sprints. You go as hard as you possibly can for a short burst. This is great for the end of a race. Second are runs. This should be a challenging pace but one you can maintain for a few minutes. Next are jogging segments. These are slower. Fourth are walking segments. No, they are not optional. Even if you think you can run the whole time without trouble, you still need to take walk breaks when I call them out during this drill. Is that understood?"

The team members nodded and said yes.

"OK," Coach Henry said. "Each segment will take a different amount of time, and they won't always go in order from one to four. You'll have to listen for my whistle and then hear me call out the pace you need to go. Ready?"

"Yes," the team said.

"I can't hear you!" Coach yelled.

"Yes!" they shouted. Everyone got up from the grass and headed to the starting line of the track.

"Starting with a jog," Coach Henry shouted. "Take your mark, get set, go!"

Alvin burst out with all the energy he could muster. *This isn't a long run. It's a drill,* he thought. *I don't have to conserve energy.*

He easily got to the front of the pack, in line with Emilio and Oscar. His feet slapped on the ground as he tried to keep up.

Emilio looked over. "You're going too fast, Braga," he said. "When I get to *my* sprint, you're going to be tired. You have no idea what you're doing. I don't understand why you're even on this team."

"Shut up," Alvin said. "I'm faster than you, and you know it."

"Only when you're sprinting," Emilio said. "I was second in the state last year, and I'm going to be first this year. When we're at our first meet, I bet you're going to fall on your face."

Alvin tried to think of a comeback, but Coach Henry was blowing his whistle. "Run!" Emilio and Oscar left him behind.

Emilio's right, Alvin realized. *I'm already tired.*

He slowed down a little, but he was breathing hard. Most of the team caught up with him. He didn't want anyone to think he was weak, so he kept going. They had to be due for a walk any second now.

He was wrong. The whistle blew again. "Sprint!"

It sounded like an elephant stampede, as everyone barreled ahead. Alvin knew this was his time to shine, but he couldn't go any faster. He was too tired.

Thankfully it was only ten seconds. "Jog!" called Coach Henry.

Alvin slowed down even more. He changed his breathing to the pattern that Neela had shared with Arianna on the first day of practicing as a group. *In, in, out, out,* he thought with each step. He started to feel better.

"Walk!" called the coach.

Alvin took long, slow strides to slow down to his walk. *Finally!*

Arianna caught up with him. "Hey!" she said brightly. For someone who was supposed to be slow like him, she barely seemed out of breath. Alvin was beginning to see why pacing mattered.

"Hey," he said hoarsely.

"Tired?" She grinned, but kindly.

"Yep," Alvin admitted. "I went too fast at the beginning."

"I noticed," Arianna said. "You really like sprinting."

"I love it!" Alvin said. "I thought cross country would be more like that."

"Can't sprint across the whole country in thirty seconds," Arianna joked.

"Ha!" Alvin couldn't help but smile.

Coach Henry blew the whistle. "Run!"

"Let's go!" said Arianna. They both sped up, keeping pace with each other. *Boomboomboomboomboom* went their feet.

Alvin looked around. They were in the middle of the pack, and he could see Neela just ahead of them.

"Jog!" *Boom, boom, boom* went their sneakers.

A minute later, the whistle blew again. "Run!"

Then, a minute later, "Jog!"

Another minute later, "Run!"

"This is getting repetitive," Arianna said.

"It is," Alvin agreed. At least they had caught up with Neela.

At the next whistle, Coach Henry finally shouted out another walk break. "You're doing better,"

Arianna said. "I was wondering why Coach Henry put us in pacing groups last week, but now I get it. We can help each other stay on track. No pun intended," she added, pointing to the track they were running on.

"Yeah," Neela said. "We can help you with your pacing, and you can help us challenge ourselves. Once I find my pace I have a hard time changing it, but sometimes you do need to speed up at the end."

"I can definitely help you with *that*," Alvin said with a grin.

"Run!" Coach Henry called. Alvin hadn't even heard the whistle.

Emilio jogged past them. "Which one of them's your girlfriend, Alvin?"

"Some of us who aren't jerks have real friends, Emilio! We don't all have huge heads like you," Neela shot back.

Alvin realized that Emilio had a habit of being disrespectful to the girls on the team, but only some of the boys—like Alvin. Then Alvin thought about how he had reacted to being put in a group with Arianna and Neela. And here they were defending him and their group.

"Hey," Alvin said the next time they had a walk break. "I'm sorry I was so mean when we first got put in a group. I shouldn't have said that we shouldn't be in a group together just because you were girls."

"That wasn't cool," Neela said. "But I guess we can forgive you. You agree, Arianna?"

"I guess so," Arianna teased. "But don't let it happen again."

After a few seconds, Coach Henry called for a twenty-second sprint. They reduced to a twenty-second run, and they repeated that two more times. During the third round, Alvin realized that even though he was tired, his shins weren't hurting like they had last week. His breathing had improved too. He could take deep breaths without gulping so much.

Coach Henry blew the whistle. "Walk!" Everyone slowed down, and even Emilio, who had lapped nearly everyone, looked like he needed the break. After two minutes of walking, Coach Henry blew the whistle once more. "Bring it in!"

Half the team jogged back, while the rest kept walking. Neela caught up with Arianna and Alvin, and the three of them walked back together.

"Whew!" Neela said. "That was exhausting."

"I know!" Alvin said.

"Hey, I was thinking," Arianna said. "We should exchange phone numbers. Maybe we can get together sometime and run on our own."

"Or sit on a couch and relax," Alvin said.

"I like Alvin's idea!" said Neela.

"Well, either one works for me," Arianna said. "After practice, make sure you wait so we can get our phones. Coach Henry won't be happy if we pull them out while we're having a team meeting."

"Great!" said Neela. She looked at Alvin with a big smile on her face. He smiled back. Maybe his group *was* the right one for him.

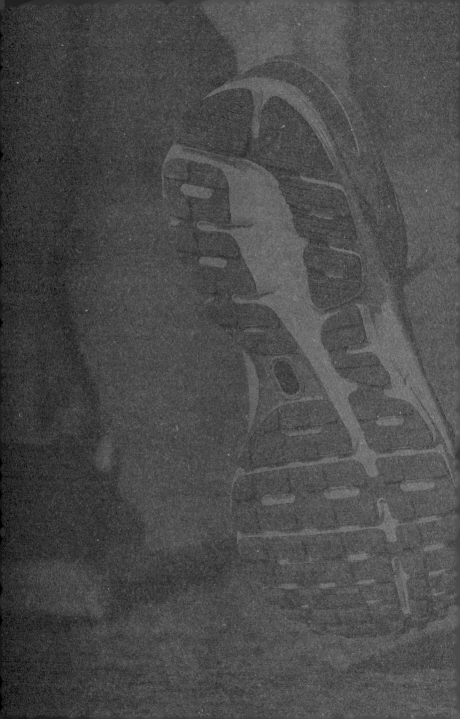

CHAPTER 8

RUN FOR FUN

That weekend, Neela texted Alvin and Arianna. *Wanna go for a run?* her text said. Alvin had finished his homework already, so he texted back that he was in. Arianna agreed too.

There were lots of paths for walking and running that snaked throughout Alvin's neighborhood, so he invited them to meet there. An hour later, both girls arrived.

The three set out. Alvin described the neighborhood path to his running partners. "How many miles is it?" Neela asked.

"I don't actually know," Alvin said. "I've never needed to know before. I guess we'll find out!"

"I'm going to set the GPS on my watch," Neela said. "That way we can keep track of how many miles we're doing."

They did some of the warm-up exercises Coach Henry had them do at practices. Then they set off at an easy jog.

* * *

At three miles, Alvin was surprised to find that he really was having a good time. Even though the first mile had felt pretty long, he had settled into the running. He was feeling light on his feet, like he could go for miles and miles more. It was the first time that he'd enjoyed running at a steady pace.

Nobody talked. They just stayed in pace with each other as they ran through the neighborhood, looking at the scenery around them. As they ran, they dodged some dog walkers and strollers on the winding route.

It felt like only a few minutes before Neela said, "My mom will be coming soon. We should head back."

"But we haven't been out that long!" Alvin said. "I thought she said she wouldn't be back until five."

Arianna looked at her phone. "It's 4:45."

Really? Alvin thought. *We've been running a long time!*

"How many miles did we do, Neela?" he asked.

"Almost eight," she said. "So we might go a little bit over that to get back to your house, Alvin."

Alvin had never run that far. They couldn't run that kind of distance at practice. There wasn't enough time between warm-ups and drills and when they had to go home again.

"I guess pacing myself can be just as good as going fast, because that felt great," Alvin said. "We should do that again."

"Just not tomorrow!" Neela said. "My legs need a break."

"Maybe next weekend?" Arianna suggested.

They agreed and raced back to Alvin's house.

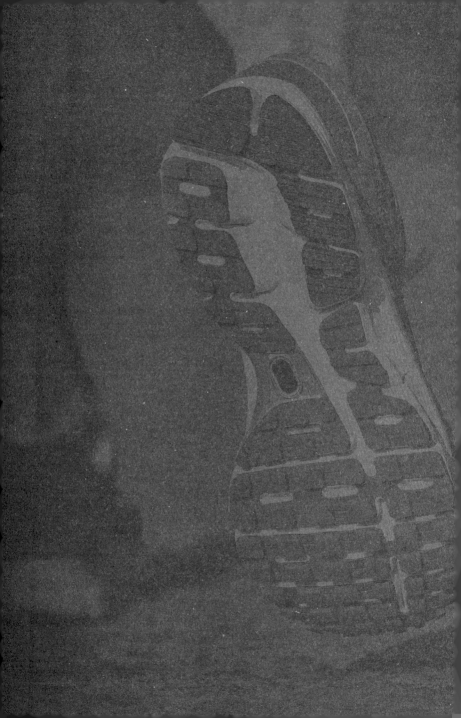

CHAPTER 9

CROSS-TRAINING

On Monday it was rainy, so practice was moved to the cafeteria. All the tables were folded up and pushed against the wall.

"Are we running inside?" someone asked.

"It's too small a space," Coach Henry said. "Today we're going to do some cross-training."

"What's cross-training?" Alvin asked.

"It means doing a different kind of exercise now and again to give your body a new challenge. It rests some of your running muscles and trains others so your body stays in balance and can support you as you run," the coach said. "Everybody, stand up."

Coach Henry led everyone in some of the same warm-up exercises they did when they were outside. Then he showed everyone how to do a proper squat.

"Imagine you have a chair behind you," Coach said. "You want to drive your hips back so that you can sit in that chair. Make sure your knees are tracking over your feet." He showed everyone two more squats. Then he walked through the room, helping everyone perfect their form.

When Coach got to Alvin, the young runner already knew what he was going to hear. "Slow down, Alvin," Coach Henry said. "It's not about how many you can do, but how well you can do them."

Squats seemed easy to Alvin at first. But once he took the time to listen to Coach Henry's directions, he realized they were much more challenging. Coach Henry had him take four counts just to go all the way down and then two counts to get back up. Alvin could feel the front of his thighs burning by the time Coach moved them on to another exercise.

After they had done squats, lunges, calf raises, and crunches, they spread out all over the room. "Push-ups!" Coach Henry announced. "Let me show you a perfect one first."

He knelt to the ground and then pushed himself into a strong plank position. With his elbows tucked in at his sides, Coach Henry lowered himself down with control and then pushed himself back up.

"I want you all to try for ten," Coach Henry said.

As Alvin knelt down to the floor, he looked over to his right. Just his luck—Emilio was right next to him. Emilio looked over at Alvin and smirked. "Bet mine are better than yours," he said.

Alvin looked the other way. *Just ignore bullies,* he told himself.

"Wonderful, Neela!" he heard Coach say. "Everybody, take a look over at Neela. You see how she holds her body in the same position on her way down and up, without arching her back? That's what I want to see from everybody."

"She's probably doing girl push-ups," Emilio said under his breath. He meant push-ups on the knees, which were still challenging when you did them right.

Alvin glanced over at Neela. He could see that she was incredibly strong, doing all of her push-ups on her toes, like Coach had demonstrated. She finished her ten and didn't break a sweat. Most of the rest of the team looked on in awe.

"Take a bow, Neela!" Coach said. Neela smiled but looked embarrassed at the attention. "Now, everyone else, finish yours!"

Alvin concentrated, not on doing his push-ups quickly but trying to match Coach's—and Neela's—push-ups exactly. He focused on keeping his form controlled while going down and up. Though the last one ached a bit, he finished.

As he rested, he looked back over at Emilio. Coach Henry was leaning over Emilio, correcting his form. "Slower," he was saying. "No—don't arch your back like that. Flat back." Soon everyone had finished their push-ups, and Coach was still working with Emilio to complete one perfectly.

When he had finally satisfied Coach Henry, Emilio stood up and saw that everyone was looking at him. He looked Alvin right in the eye. Alvin could tell he was embarrassed. He knew if it were him in Emilio's place, Emilio would have said something mean.

Instead, Alvin looked Emilio back in the eye but said nothing. Emilio glared.

Coach Henry watched the two boys. When he saw neither of them was going to say anything, he clapped his hands together. "OK, everyone! We're going to run through all those exercises again."

There was a loud groan throughout the cafeteria. Coach Henry chuckled. "You'll be glad of it when you realize how much stronger your muscles are after this," he said.

The coach divided them into two teams. "For this second round, we're going to make it a tag-team challenge. Each person on your team has to do each exercise before you move on to the next exercise. Let's see who can move through the exercises the fastest."

As the competition got under way, the room grew loud. Alvin looked over his team. Arianna and Neela were on the other side, so Alvin knew his team could be in for a challenge when they got to push-ups.

Even worse, Emilio was on Alvin's team. "Come on, people! You're going too slow," the upperclassman complained as his team did the squats. Emilio approached Coach Henry. "Coach, your teams aren't fair. We have too many girls to win."

"Emilio, that's enough out of you," Coach said. "Just worry about your own exercises."

As Emilio frowned, Alvin turned his attention back to the competition. "Go, Tom!" *Clap, clap.* "Go, Tom!" *Clap, clap.* Alvin began chanting for a teammate doing lunges. The rest of his teammates except Emilio joined in. Then the other side started their own chant.

Both teams continued the cheer for each teammate throughout the competition, erupting in laughter by the end of the contest. Alvin's team lost, but just barely.

When practice ended, Alvin was sore, and he knew everyone else was too. But they were all smiling. Somehow, being inside and not running had helped the team come together. Alvin realized something: *I do want to be on this team. I want to learn how to run for long distances.*

Now he just had to get ready for the meet at the end of the week.

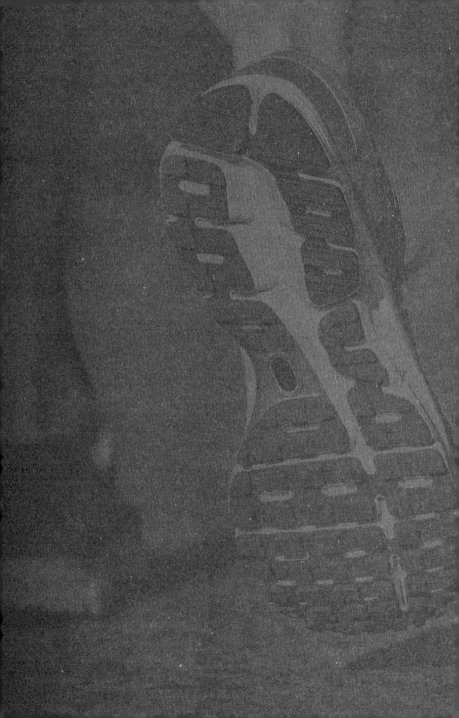

CHAPTER 10

FIRST RACE

The meet was between four middle schools. There was one event: the 2.1-mile race. There were so many runners and not a lot of space on the course, so the boys and girls were each divided into two heats.

Alvin was in the second boys heat. Emilio was in the first. When the buzzer sounded, he saw the runners take off, and Emilio was in the middle of the pack.

Ha! Alvin thought. *He's not the fastest of them all.*

The race was two laps around the field, and soon the runners were coming back around to start their second lap. Emilio was still in the middle, but he was pulling ahead.

Alvin watched him closely. At practices, Emilio often had a smile or a smirk on his face. But now he was concentrating hard, and his chest was tall and open. He took long, even strides, not quick and heavy ones like Alvin often did.

When they had half a lap to go, Emilio was in second place. Alvin hadn't even noticed him speed up. Now Emilio was leaning forward, and his strides were getting shorter. He was beginning to sprint so that he could catch the last runner ahead of him.

The crowd began to cheer as the race neared its end. Emilio and a boy from another school were head-to-head. Oscar was in third place. Just a few yards from the finish line, Emilio burst ahead, a look of determination on his face. He won, with the other boy a split second behind him.

Alvin's team cheered as loud as they could.

There were only a few minutes for everyone to clear out so the second heat could start. The girls had already gone, so it was the last race of the day.

The crowd had cleared out some, but there were still a lot of parents and a few teachers from the host school. Alvin's dad was there too.

When the buzzer sounded, Alvin took off as he usually did, immediately making it to the front. He stayed there for nearly the entire first lap, until he recognized that dull pain in his shins. *Slow down!* he imagined Coach Henry saying. *Pace yourself!*

He remembered how Emilio, fast as he was, had stayed in the middle of the group until the second mile. He took a deep breath, lifted his chest, and slowed down.

Soon other runners had caught up to him, but he tried not to let it bother him. He concentrated on feeling his feet hit the ground, one after the other.

It felt like forever, but finally Alvin made it to the end. He looked behind him. There were three runners to go.

He jumped for joy. He knew he wouldn't get a medal, but he had finished the race.

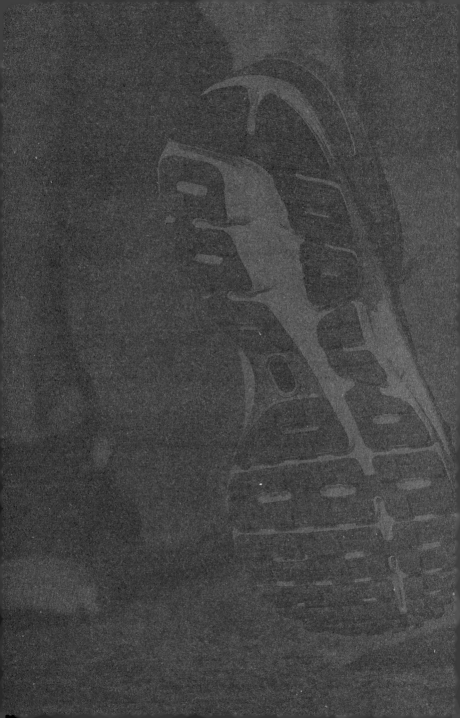

CHAPTER 11

ALL IN

At the next practice, Coach Henry called Alvin over. "I was proud of how you ran your first race," he said. "You had the best form you've had all season, and you showed restraint. I think you'll have a great running career if you keep working on your pacing."

Alvin beamed. "Thanks, Coach!"

He ran back to join the team as they worked on hill repeats. Those still made him tired, but he hadn't had shin splints since the meet.

They ended the practice with a one-mile run. This time, Alvin didn't worry about being first.

He didn't even worry about keeping up with Arianna and Neela. He just kept repeating to himself all the things Coach Henry had been telling him all season: *head up, chest out, no fists, light on your feet.*

He stopped paying attention for a moment and tripped forward. As he regained his balance, he leaned forward again in his usual sprint.

"Slow down, Braga!" he heard Coach Henry shout.

Head up! Look forward! Alvin said to himself.

Emilio caught up to Alvin. "Hey," he said.

Alvin didn't want to hear Emilio make another joke at his expense. "Lay off, Emilio," he said.

Emilio put his hands up. "Hey, I was just going to say you're doing better. It took me a while to lap you this time."

"Yeah, yeah."

"Look, Coach tells me that if I want to be a leader on this team, I have to do more than run fast. So I'm trying to be more . . . encouraging, or whatever," said Emilio.

"So you're being nice because you have to?" asked Alvin.

Emilio ignored the question. "You're only a seventh grader, and you didn't run last year. I didn't place at all the first year I ran in sixth grade. Not at a single meet."

That was surprising to Alvin. "Really?"

"Really," Emilio confirmed.

They slowed down so they could talk without running out of breath.

"Don't expect any medals or anything, but don't worry about it too much either," said Emilio. "And Coach says I should apologize. So I'm sorry if I've been a jerk. I just like joking around."

"Your jokes aren't very funny," said Alvin. After a moment, he added, "You're especially mean to the girls. It's not cool. The girls work as hard as we do."

"You might be right about that." Emilio shrugged his shoulders and added, "Who knows? Maybe Coach Henry will have me apologize to them next. Anyway, peace out!" Emilio picked up his speed and left Alvin in the dust.

* * *

It was the last meet of the season. Alvin's parents had both arranged to be there. Today was Alvin's day.

There were two races—2.1 miles and one mile. Alvin was running the mile. When it was his turn, he found a place at the starting line.

The buzzer sounded, and he waited a split second to let the other runners go. He wanted a little space to himself. He started in a jog, remembering to conserve his energy. Slowly he picked up his pace to a run and caught up to the middle of the pack of runners.

The race was only one lap, and he didn't want to fall too far behind. Instead of going into a sprint, he made each stride slightly shorter than the one before it until he was going just under a sprint speed. There was about a quarter of a mile left, and he was nearly to the front.

He looked out to the crowd for a moment. He couldn't find his parents, but he knew they were there watching.

With just a few yards to go, Alvin knew it was time to go all in. He picked up his pace and sprinted, pulling ahead of one of the boys from the other school. He barely had any breath left. But he drew up energy he didn't know he had, and he ran for the finish line thinking of nothing else.

There were cheers all over. Alvin slowed to a jog and then a walk, looking around. How had he done?

"Alvin!" Arianna and Neela were running up to him. Alvin raised both arms and each girl high-fived one hand.

"That was awesome!" Arianna said.

"Thanks," Alvin said. He couldn't stop smiling. "You two were great too. Congratulations on your silver, Neela!"

"Thank you!" Neela said. "I am really proud of myself—and of Arianna. She had a really close race."

"I think we can agree that we're all awesome," Arianna said.

There were lots of people gathering on the field. Alvin felt a hand on his shoulder. It was Coach Henry.

"Great work, Alvin! Fantastic," he said.

Alvin grinned. "Really?"

"Really," Coach Henry said. "Your form was great, and you paced yourself until the very end. That was an awesome sprint. I'm really proud of you. You earned that bronze."

Bronze?

A woman with a bullhorn stood in the middle of the field announcing names. Alvin heard two names for first and second, and then his name was called. A man put the bronze medal over Alvin's head.

Coach Henry had a huge smile on his face. "Go find your family," he said. "They're going to congratulate you."

Alvin looked over at the bleachers. He didn't see them.

Then all of a sudden they were right in front of him. And not just his parents—Yasmin was there too!

"Great work, Alv!" Mom said.

"We knew you could do it," said Dad.

"Thanks," Alvin said. They pulled him into a hug.

After they released him, Alvin looked at his twin sister. "What are you doing here?" he asked.

"I told the director I needed to leave rehearsal early today," she said. "I wanted to come support my brother."

Alvin smiled and gave his sister a sweaty hug.

"Eww, stop!" she cried.

Alvin let her go. "Thanks for coming, Yasmin."

"Of course. Are you OK with third place?" Yasmin asked.

"Are you OK with your understudy taking over for you for one rehearsal?" Alvin replied.

Yasmin laughed. "I think I can handle it."

"Well, I think I can handle this too," Alvin said, looking at his medal. "Today, third feels like first."

ABOUT the AUTHOR

Sarah Hannah Gómez has a masters of art degree in children's literature and masters of science in library science. She is now a writer and fitness instructor in Tucson, Arizona. She is working toward a doctoral degree in children's literature at the University of Arizona. Find her online at shgmclicious.com.

GLOSSARY

baseline (BAYSS-line)—a basic standard or level

contract (KON-trakt)—an agreement between people that states what each party agrees to do

drill (DRILL)—a physical exercise that's practiced over and over

extracurricular (ek-struh-kuh-RIK-yuh-ler)—related to activities that are offered by a school but are not part of the coursework

gender (JEN-der)—the state of being either male or female

meet (MEET)—a sports contest

pace (PAYSS)—rate of speed while running

plank (PLANGK)—an exercise that involves steadily holding the body off the ground in a position similar to a push-up, on either the hands or elbows, for as long as possible

stride (STRIDE)—a step or the distance covered by a step

time trial (TIME TRYE-uhl)—a test of an athlete's individual speed over a set distance

DISCUSSION QUESTIONS

1. In this story, Alvin tries something new. Is it easy for him to learn how to run cross country? Support your answers with details from the book. What are the pros and cons of learning a new way of doing things?

2. What has Emilio said to upset Alvin and the girls on the cross country team? Do you think this is bullying? Have you experienced bullying at school or elsewhere?

3. Alvin starts out thinking running is an individual sport. At the end of the story, what has he learned about being part of a team? What have you learned about teamwork from the story?

WRITING PROMPTS

1. Imagine that you see Emilio bullying your teammates. Write a paragraph about how you think you would address Emilio's behavior. What would you say? What would you do? Why?

2. Write about a cross country practice from Arianna or Neela's point of view. How does she see Alvin? What does she think? How does she feel?

3. Think about your favorite sport or an activity you love. Now write about how you felt and what you did when you first started. Were you good right away? Was it hard to learn? Why?

MORE ABOUT CROSS COUNTRY RUNNING

What IS Cross Country Running?

Cross country running is outdoor distance racing. It takes place on unpaved ground, paths, and trails rather than tracks. Cross country runners in teams receive points for their finishing places. The first-place finisher gets one point. The fifth-place finisher gets five points. This means the team with the lowest point score wins!

Here are more cross country facts.

Early 1800s
Cross country races were first run in England. Runners then truly ran across the countryside. They had to splash through streams, jump over fences and barriers, and even crash through hedges!

Early 1900s
Cross country running made it to the Summer Olympic Games! But . . . it was removed later because it wasn't considered a true summer sport.

1938

The NCAA National Championship Races for men held its first meet. It wasn't until . . .

1981

. . . that the NCAA Women's National Championship Race took place.

226,000

This is how many cross country runners continue to compete through high school in the United States. Cross country is the sixth most popular girls' and the seventh most popular boys' school sport.

6.2

This is the maximum number of miles in a men's college cross country race, and . . .

3.7

. . . this is the maximum number of miles in a women's college cross country race.

$30,000

This is the prize money the first-place winner in the individual senior race of the 2017 IAAF World Cross Country Championships received. So . . . keep running! You never know how far cross country can take you.